Goat Mountain

Habib Selmi

Goat Mountain

Translated from the Arabic
by Charis Olszok

Banipal Books

Goat Mountain is first published in English
translation by Banipal Books, London 2020

Arabic Copyright © 2020 Habib Selmi
Translation Copyright © 2020 Charis Olszok

First published in Arabic as
جبل العنز (Jabal al-Anz), by Arab Institute
for Research & Publishing, Beirut, 1988

The moral rights of Habib Selmi to be identified
as the author of these works and of Charis Olszok
to be identified as the translator of this work have
been asserted in accordance with the Copyright,
Designs and Patents Act, 1988.

No part of this book may be reproduced in any
form or by any means without the prior written
permission of the publisher

Cover photo: a Tunisian desert village

A CIP record for *Goat Mountain* is available
in the British Library
ISBN 978-1-913043-04-9
E-book: ISBN: 978-1-913043-05-6

Banipal Books
1 Gough Square, LONDON EC4A 3DE, UK
www.banipal.co.uk/banipalbooks/

Banipal Books is an imprint
of Banipal Publishing

Set in Bembo

Goat Mountain

JAMES KIRKUP

The intense, glacial fantasy that is *Goat Mountain*

This brief, stark and finally terrifying tale begins at home, on the eve of a son's first departure for an obscure teaching post in a remote country school – a favourite theme in modern French literature also. It is a departure made with his father's prayers and blessings and a mother's joyful pride in her son's first appointment, mingled with their sadness at the prospect of a long parting.

The journey begins, like so many African journeys, in a dilapidated old bus that takes four hours to reach Al-'Ala, from where the young man takes a long ride on mule back, accompanied by a mysterious older man who is to play an important part in the young man's new life. As they proceed along desert tracks under a broiling sun, the youth begins to feel the first vague apprehensions about his silent companion. They make a brief halt at a solitary carob tree, where the man tells him seven men, including his own grandfather, had been murdered on the orders of the Pasha for taking part in an uprising against taxes. The young man begins to feel not just fear, but also an indefinable hatred for this "man about whom I knew nothing, except that he was the grandson of a rebel slaughtered in an obscure, mysterious land". Thus the whole atmosphere of brooding horror and senseless violence is perfectly evoked in this first chapter, written like all the others in a spare, plain, factual yet strangely haunting style, with a secret poetic undercurrent that once or twice reminds us of Camus at his best. We remember the author's epigraph from Pessóa's *Book of Disquiet*: "We all live anonymously and apart from one another; in disguise, we suffer yet remain unknown . . ."

They finally arrive at Jabal al-'Anz – Goat Mountain – a forlorn, dusty desert village. The school is a single room. The youth passes the first night in the house of his uncommunicative guide, whose name is Ismail. The house is surprisingly well kept, with a large shelf of books: history, literature, Islamic law and Qur'anic exegesis. Next morning, they return to the school, where Ismail shows the young man his living quarters, a small room behind the class. Ismail tells him: "If you need anything, please inform me. I am the government's representative in Goat Mountain."

It is the beginning of a very strange sort of love-hate relationship between the two men – not exactly friends, but not yet enemies, either. Their association is composed of both elements, of which the sense of enmity begins to be the stronger. An increasingly unbearable tension develops between them, which is reflected in the life of the village. The young man grows more uneasy and depressed as Ismail becomes ever more powerful until, with a new truck and his own private army, he dominates village life and casts a menacing shadow over the young man until the latter reaches the verge of paranoia and madness.

This intense, glacial fantasy is the work of a literary master. At a subliminal level, it can be read as the intellectual's despairing and suicidal attack on inhuman political power. It reminded me of the writings of two Africans I have translated: Camara Laye and Tierno Monénembo. From the latter's brave novel *Les Crapauds-brousse* we learn the nickname taxis-brousse, given to all forms of primitive local long-distance transport, usually open trucks, or at best buses, like the one in Habib Selmi's story.

Reproduced from
Banipal No 6, Autumn 1999

1

In all honesty, I was not as thrilled as I had expected to be. A slight tremor ran through me but nothing more. Then again, I have always been that way. I become feverishly engrossed, my entire being absorbed. But soon I lose interest and end up feeling hollow and empty. The truth is that I combine many such contradictions imperceptible to all but me: headstrong but ambivalent, level-headed but flighty. Do I deliberately conceal them? Perhaps. I have a capacity for dissimulation which sometimes takes even me by surprise. That day, I read my letter of appointment twice: first when I received it and later when I withdrew to the solitude of my room.

That evening my brother played quietly and happily, and as my father performed the sunset prayer I felt that he was, for the first time, reciting the *fatiha* at ease, relishing every word. The scent of grass drifted through the open windows, accompanied by the gentle croak of frogs and a trill in the distance, echoing like a woman's mournful wail. Goat Mountain. I do not deny that it was the name itself that had intrigued me, and, without giving a thought to the actual place, a mammoth-like goat, with long, thick legs and a great udder swollen with milk enough to nourish the entire village had materialised before my eyes. What other reason could there be for that name?

Bleached animal bones lay at the bottom of steep slopes. The bus was pungent with the scent of juniper and the wheels rumbled as it laboured up the sharp rises. Stretching out to east and west were endless expanses of tall dry grass and pine forests. In a fleeting dream, I saw myself sinking slowly but surely into a coffee-coloured land, oozing mud.

My fellow passengers kept to themselves, seated as far from one another as possible. They had the mournful, reticent look of contagious invalids on their way to quarantine. Leaning back, I glimpsed the pallid features of my own face reflected in the spattered window pane.

After four hours, the bus pulled into a marketplace lined with wooden stalls. The engine grew silent.

"Al-'Ala!" the driver called, preparing to descend.

The passengers surged towards the door and disappeared into the darkness while other men, who I later learned were merchants, surrounded the bus, electric torches in hands. Others still, barefoot and girded with leather belts, clambered on board and began unloading wares amidst the clamour and the cries.

The following morning, Al-'Ala village appeared larger than it had done the previous night. I was escorted by the bus driver to one of the shopkeepers who greeted me warmly and instructed me to follow him. We crossed the square at the far side of which stood a dusty tree, encircled by an iron railing. At the end of the row of stalls, we found ourselves surrounded by several houses with low doors. In a corner, a pair of goats stood tied to a metal ring and beside them mules were grazing on straw. I remained motionless, completely absorbed by the sight of the goats, one of which was endowed with a startlingly large udder. The merchant, who had gone into one of the houses, emerged with a smile on his face.

"Stay here," he ordered me.

As I watched him disappear, I reflected on how lucky I was.

My mother had said so too, weeping with joy at the news of my appointment. Later, after staunching her tears, she had reminisced about events from my childhood, grown hazy in my memory.

★ ★ ★

A voice drifted from the house, muffled as though it were coming from underground. The scent of moisture and damp straw hung in the air. As I walked towards the building, I had the distinct impression of approaching a holy shrine. Crossing the threshold, this impression increased as I found myself in a room, its floor covered in mats and its corners shrouded in darkness. A man was kneeling motionless on an old rug, a pitcher of water to his right. He was facing a wall on which hung a small lamp, its light reflected by the surrounding stone. I retreated and the man immediately rose to his feet and followed me out. I remember his smile clearly. It was a broad, friendly smile but something about it disturbed me, though I was incapable of saying what. He saddled two mules and we set off. Having reached the far side of the marketplace, I turned to look back and saw the shopkeeper watching us leave. I waved to him and he waved back. To this day, I feel certain that he still remembers me.

After leaving the village, we mounted the mules, crossing through wide fields and trotting past shuttered houses and farmers herding their livestock. My companion stared straight ahead, thrusting his chin forward every now and then to indicate the direction. I glanced at his face, observing his wide dark eyes, ruddy lips and short hair, parted neatly down the middle with a precision that suggested an inordinate amount of care.

Having reached the top of a sandy rise, we began to descend the other side and I was forced to pull tightly on my reins and sit bolt upright for fear of falling from my mount. As I did so, the man turned to me.

"Be careful," he murmured, "The path's bumpy."

The sun rose in a crystal clear sky and my body began to trickle with sweat. During the first stretch of our journey, we occasionally glimpsed men on mules and donkeys, conversing with one another in raised voices that drifted to us in the distance. Then, quite suddenly, we were confronted by nothingness. The ground stretched into the distance, bare but for several lone shrubs. The sound of the mules' hooves striking rhythmically on the ground rang clearly in my ears, lulling me to sleep. Although it was still morning, the heat was intense. As I raised my face to the sky, I felt as though we were the sole recipients of the sun's infernal blaze. Every particle of its heat seemed to be bearing down on us and us alone. My hands began to slacken and, every now and then, I was forced to release my grip on the reins so as to wipe drops of sweat from my eyes. Since receiving my letter of appointment, I had not once thought about what Goat Mountain might actually be like. How could this have escaped me? I gazed around at the silent, rosy landscape. For the first time I felt fear, tinged with regret, and heightened by the silence of the man leading me through that vast emptiness to an unknown destination. He remained taciturn, rigid on his mule as though fastened to it by leather straps.

We crossed a parched valley fringed by oleanders. The hooves of our mules sunk swiftly into the deep sand which bore no trace of man or animal as though we were the first to set foot on its virgin surface. The man tugged on his reins, halting his mule by a carob tree that rose up incongruously in the arid landscape. I assumed he intended to rest but he remained motionless, gazing at the tree as though seeing it for the first time.

Then, without turning to me, he spoke:

"Here, seven men were slaughtered, their corpses left for the crows." He dismounted and began stirring the sand with his foot.

"Here they lie," he repeated, "here they lie."

"Who slaughtered them?"

"The Pasha," he murmured, as though to himself.

He stood tense and unmoving, then, stretching out his hands and closing his eyes, several tears slid down his cheeks. As though sensing my discomfort, he brushed them brusquely away.

"My grandfather was among those men."

"Why were they killed?"

"For rebelling against the taxes," he replied after a

short silence, speaking low as though divulging a secret.

He paused again, before embarking on a long speech, in which, with increasing relish, he described his grandfather who had married three times and fathered eighteen sons. Five of them had travelled to the city and lost all contact with home. Others had died in tribal wars.

At first, his speech captivated me and I began to picture the corpses decomposing beneath the blazing sun. Then, quite at random, I felt a wave of hatred rise within me, prompted by his tears. As I watched him, his face began to change, his features blurring into those of my father. This was a man about whom I knew nothing, except that he was the grandson of a rebel slaughtered in an obscure, mysterious land.

As we progressed steadily up a steep rise, the rocks around us multiplied and the path became too narrow for the mules to walk side by side. We moved forward in single file. Then, wending our way down the other side, we reached a small stream. Without a word, we pulled our mules simultaneously to a halt and dismounted.

The man seated himself on the bank while I plunged my head into the water before scooping it up and splashing it onto my chest. I finally decided to immerse myself entirely, sinking happily under. Watching me, the man laughed.

"And what will you do in Goat Mountain?" he asked.

His question troubled me, perhaps because he had not asked it straight away. I stopped splashing and, for a moment, considered not replying. Then, looking him squarely in the eyes, I answered.

"I will teach the children."

Without a word, he looked away then rose to his feet and mounted his mule.

"So now they're worried about the children . . ." he said, his voice dripping with sarcasm as we set off once again.

2

Goat Mountain was not large. In the afternoons, dust started to swirl, dying down only at nightfall when the bats began their tireless circling. The school consisted of a single classroom, which could hold up to thirty children. In its courtyard stood a mulberry tree, which the residents of Goat Mountain estimated to be around three hundred years old although they did not know who had planted it originally.

We arrived shortly after midday, passing by houses where naked children peeped through doorways. A crowd of men came to walk alongside us, peering intently up at me as though I had descended from some alien planet. At the far end of the village, on a slight rise, my companion halted his mule in front of a small house built and we dismounted. One of the men led the mules off to be watered and fed. I hovered, unsure what to do next, stripped of volition before the sea of enquiring eyes fixed upon me.

"This is the school," the man said, gesturing towards the building.

On hearing this, the men began muttering knowingly to one another and some of them broke into broad smiles before eventually heading off on their separate errands. I am certain that the villagers will continue to talk of me for years to come as they harvest their potatoes, disagreeing between themselves as they carry on talking about the appearance of the mule I rode that day.

I spent the first night with my companion whose name, I learned, was Ismail. Even as I walked through the door, I was struck by the cleanliness of his house, boldly defying the sandstorms which visited the village every afternoon without fail. The furniture was arranged with painstaking precision, but what truly astonished me was the tall wooden bookcase on which large leather-bound volumes were stacked. Without asking permission, I headed straight to it, unable to rein in my curiosity, and began flicking through the tomes of Qur'anic exegesis, history, Islamic law and literature. Ismail turned to me, his lips curved into a smile.

"Those belonged to my grandfather."

I continued leafing through them.

"He was a great scholar," he added. "He studied at the Zaytuna University for two years but had to leave early because his father couldn't afford the fees."

The next morning we went to the school. Ismail headed straight to the back of the classroom, weaving his way through the scattered wooden chairs towards a low door which had I overlooked on my first visit.

"This is your new home," he announced, opening the door. "If you need anything, please inform me. I am the government's representative in Goat Mountain." Astonished by his words, I stood motionless and suddenly the image of him standing beneath the carob tree, weeping for a grandfather long dead, flashed through my mind.

My home was made ready in a single day; the spiders webs obliterated, the walls painted and the door and windows polished. Years later, as I watched the noontide light filtering through the small window of my cell, I recalled the first moments of my life in that house.

★ ★ ★

I spent the first days alone, keeping to myself. At nightfall, I would light my lantern and compose long letters to my family, telling them how the residents of Goat Mountain grew exceptional potatoes, how their children were intelligent and how terribly alone I felt. Their letters always took a long time to reach me. I would wait expectantly for the day when Ismail went to collect them from Al-'Ala, the last delivery point.

Within a short space of time, we grew very close. He introduced me to every family in the village, taking me round from house to house. But, in spite of that, I remained wary of him. Whenever we passed the mulberry tree, he would assure me that it was his grandfather who had planted it. He had bought the seedling in the city, Ismail told me, and, as it grew, he had built protective fencing around it to guard it from the cows and goats. It was he who had pruned it back every year and this, Ismail asserted, entitled him to exclusive rights over its fruits.

The isolation that he occasionally imposed on himself also intrigued me. For days on end he would remain in his house, talking to no one. In order to save money so as to accomplish his grandfather's dying wish, he often consumed only boiled potatoes, larks caught in snares or wild plants uprooted from the vegetation surrounding his house. On other occasions, however, he would embark on a lavish shopping spree in Al-'Ala, returning laden with shoes, socks, trousers and saddlebags stuffed with tins of his beloved sardines, as well as vials of perfume which he lined up on the bookcase. The residents of Goat Mountain observed him with ironic smiles.

"He'll meet the same end as his grandfather," they murmured to one another.

At the beginning of every month, Ismail went from house to house, noting down all new births, a pair of steel-rimmed spectacles inherited from his grandfather perched on his nose. With utmost care, he recorded the names of the babies, their fathers, mothers, grandfathers and grandmothers in an imposing logbook and, on Thursdays, he copied them into the official government files in Al-'Ala. He would often grow agitated when the new parents could not specify the exact time of birth and sometimes he would even remove the coverlet from the baby and flip it over to confirm its sex.

The citizens of Goat Mountain, he informed me, only thought of such matters when their babies had already begun to crawl around.

At the end of every month, meanwhile, Ismail would gather everyone beneath the mulberry tree and read to them from a newspaper, which was always a week out of date. After reviewing everything of import, he would tell his audience that the soil of Goat Mountain was fertile, that it produced the world's finest potatoes and that the government would soon add new rooms to the school, build a hospital, and lay a wide road through the mountains, connecting Goat Mountain to Al-'Ala. They would pave the streets and exterminate the insects and rodents, and Goat Mountain would be transformed into a great city frequented by ministers, circuses, famous bands and tourists eager to experience their exceptional potato farming.

Ismail would begin his monologue softly but his

voice grew gradually louder as he progressed, his eyes glowing and spittle flying from his mouth.

★ ★ ★

Then one day everything changed. I often try to reconstruct the exact details of the scene in my head. At first, it remains hazy but I pursue it stubbornly until I can almost inhale the scent of the wooden chairs. I was standing in the classroom facing the blackboard. Moving my head slightly, I caught sight of Ismail. He moved through the chairs to the back of the class and took a seat. That night I found him at home, totally absorbed in writing, soaking his lower legs in a bucket of water. Seeing me hovering in the doorway, he lifted his head. Fatigue was written plainly across his features. He gave a forced smile then looked down again.

"I'm writing a report about you," he said, "about your teaching."

He shifted his legs about in the bucket and gave another smile. I stood rooted to the spot, feeling a cold shiver down my spine. Saying nothing, I gazed intently at the rainbow of colours cast by his oil lamp. Ismail seemed to relax, leaning back against the wooden chair.

"You understand . . . don't you?" he asked, putting his pen down. "It's my job."

He fell silent for a moment and then continued, toying with the pen.

"I cannot remain silent . . ."

"About what?" I interrupted him.

He sprang instantly to his feet.

"Don't think me so gullible," he roared, "I know your tricks."

He fell silent. I saw his right hand slacken. He sat back on the chair, looking at me as though he would like to continue speaking.

The next time he came to the school, I stood blocking the doorway. I was furious and was determined to confront him. He did not attempt to push past me but simply grinned broadly and turned on his heel, walking slowly away and glancing left and right. I continued watching him until he had crossed the courtyard.

As he disappeared I felt as though I had won a victory, and the idea that Ismail was my enemy became embedded in my mind.

Several days later I discovered that he was no longer talking to me. My letters began to arrive later and later. I would receive only one a month. Then they stopped altogether and my isolation was complete.

It is not easy to live alone in a small village like Goat Mountain. I awoke to this reality after my initial burst of enthusiasm. I buried myself in study but could not dispel my loneliness. One night I decided not to light my lantern, and remained in darkness. Anger seized me and I tossed and turned feverishly on my mattress, sinking into a long spell of delirium. I had read and reread all the books I had brought with me and they no longer offered any respite or consolation.

Sometimes, I would spend hours tending to my hair, combing it to the right before ruffling it up and brushing it back to the left. Other times, I would clip my nails or stand in front of the mirror examining the colour of my eyes, trying to decide whether they were blue or green or yellowish green or bluish yellow. I developed strange new pastimes: counting all my notebooks with black covers and then all those with red ones; measuring the length and breadth of my bedroom; taking my razor apart and putting it together again; or simply gazing at my hands and trying to determine which was larger.

When my depression grew particularly severe I would take out my letter of appointment, contemplate it, then fold it back up and return it to its place.

During that same period, Ismail went into one of his periods of retreat. He would wake early and go for a short, lonely walk through the fields adjoining his house before disappearing inside once again.

His absence allowed me to become better acquainted with the residents of Goat Mountain. I began visiting them regularly, playing with their children and occasionally accompanying them to the fields to help dig potatoes. Little by little I overcame my loneliness and no longer worried so much about not receiving letters. I felt sure that all was well at home. I began to love Goat Mountain and soon felt as though I had been born in one of its small dwellings. The village became the centre of my universe.

3

The people of Goat Mountain grow outstanding potatoes. Digging their fingers through the freshly ploughed earth, they carefully press in each tuber before scooping earth over them with quick, deft movements. I can no longer remember why I found it so strange. It is true that I have never liked potatoes and during my stay in the village (was it three years or four?) I did not eat a single one. Their colour, however, has always intrigued me.

Many stories are told about potatoes in Goat Mountain. I listened to them intently and would write them down at night in a small notebook, which I have kept with me ever since. At first, I compared the different tales, attempting to ascertain which was most authentic. Gradually, however, I gave this up and began to love them all. They seemed to be both real and fanciful tales. When I recall them now, I allow myself to alter them slightly, embellishing them with details of my own. To a story told by an attractive widow in her fifties, known alternatively as Khadija, Bint Burawi and al-Burawiyya, I added a new beginning:

"One morning, not far from Ismail's house, we came across a new plant, ripe and green as though it had just poked through the earth. It was the children who noticed it. Pulling it from the earth, they discovered that it was not a weed as they had at first thought. They took it back to their parents who examined it closely. Several of them chewed a bit to try its flavour.

"After much discussion, they agreed that it was most likely a strange strain of colocynth with no nutritional value, especially given that neither the cattle nor the chickens would eat it and even the roosters kept their distance. They discarded the plant and its small tubers, which reminded them of partridge eggs. After some time, however, the plant reappeared. It was again the children who discovered it. A large number of the plants had spread over the ground. They gathered up the tubers, took them home and, after cooking them, discovered them to be delicious. Thus began potato fever on Goat Mountain."

I do not like the beginning of the second story and always omit it. The old man who narrated it clearly lacked imagination.

"My grandfather," he related, "was the first resident of Goat Mountain to visit the city. While there, he witnessed many remarkable things which he continued to recount to the end of his days. It was there that he discovered certain small vegetables that he ate with great delight. I remember him returning with a bag full of these potatoes and being quite incapable of defining their colour.

"God bless my grandfather. Without him, Goat Mountain would have remained in poverty."

I was told the story of the soldier on three separate occasions and can no longer remember who I heard it from first.

Forgetting the original author, however, granted my imagination free rein and I always experience immense joy when I replay it in my mind:

"One autumn evening (the story does not specify the season so I have added this small detail), a tall, green-eyed soldier arrived mysteriously in the village. He rode a beautiful chestnut horse whose snorts and whinnies filled the streets. The soldier lived in Goat Mountain for twenty years during which he taught its people to grow potatoes, led them to victory in thirteen tribal wars, built a house at the end of the village and married a woman ten years his junior who died four months after marrying him. None of the residents of Goat Mountain knew the woman's family for they lived in a distant village."

As for the house that the soldier built, according to the story it was still standing at the end of the village.

When my conflict with Ismail grew particularly bad, I left the school and took up residence there.

★ ★ ★

Dust. Barking dogs. The aroma of cooking food. Mules plodding and chickens strutting. The day of the potato market is no ordinary day in Goat Mountain for, in a village where weddings are few and far between, the people seize every opportunity for a celebration. The freshly dug potatoes are loaded into goatskin sacks or simply piled high in front of houses. At noon, the merchants arrive from Al-'Ala.

Ismail did not live off potato farming like the other villagers despite having inherited a substantial parcel of land from his grandfather. He took pride in being a government employee and in collecting a large salary on the first Thursday of every month. In some years, however, he would develop a unusual interest in his land, entrusting its cultivation to one of the villagers. Thus, it was potatoes that would end his solitude, bringing him back into the company of the people of Goat Mountain.

One day, Ismail, in his usual brusque manner, announced that he would soon journey to Mecca for Hajj. He went back and forth between Goat Mountain and Al-'Ala, preparing for his departure, then shut himself away in his house for two full days. His forthcoming pilgrimage remained the main topic of conversation in the village for quite some time. Although the people of Goat Mountain regarded many of his claims with a certain degree of scepticism, they were proud that someone from their small, forgotten village would set foot on holy ground. That season, the harvest was abundant and the earth yielded more potatoes than ever before. Even with every sack and store filled, piles of potatoes remained dotted across the fields. The children played games with them and fed them to the animals until they could manage no more.

After giving thanks to God, the villagers began to ponder the reason for such abundance. Given that the ground was the same as always and that the rainfall had been as usual, no one could help but secretly think of Ismail's Hajj.

A great surprise awaited them, however – one that the villagers had never imagined possible. A month went by and the merchants of Al-'Ala did not appear. Eventually, Ismail gathered everyone under the mulberry tree and told them that the potato harvest had been abundant everywhere that year, and farmers had ended up throwing their excess crops into the sea.

After a long silence, he added in a low voice, looking each one of them in the eye: "I have decided to buy every potato in Goat Mountain."

Shouts of joy arose, accompanied by boisterous applause. Several of the men began to dance. Ismail, meanwhile, simply reminded everyone that he was the grandson of a revolutionary who had died defending their ancestors.

4

On that afternoon of Ismail's announcement, the heat was intense and the silence oppressive. I closed the windows and door and threw myself onto my mattress. I was tired and anxious. I tried to sleep but could not and so allowed my thoughts to wander freely and randomly, something I often resort to. Attempting to forget my surroundings, I retreat into the past, playing with distant images: cows quenching their thirst at a well, children quarrelling over a dead lark or trying to forge a swollen river. Tossing and turning on the mattress, I heard the squeak of the door behind me and instantly turned over. Ismail stood on the threshold. I leapt to my feet.

"Welcome," I cried mechanically.

Ismail continued to watch me and I felt a great wave of uneasiness washing over me. I invited him in, indicating the only chair in the room.

"Sit down. Please."

He went to the chair, sweeping his gaze across the room as though searching for something. We remained in silence. Ismail stretched out his legs, revealing his sandals. I gazed fixedly at his feet and toes until he drew his legs back beneath the chair.

"It's extremely hot," I said.

He nodded in agreement and we fell silent again. I sat on the edge of the bed, wondering why he had suddenly decided to visit. He had not spoken to me since the incident at the school and had gone out of his way to isolate me and push me into leaving. While immersed in these thoughts, I heard him say:

"Have you heard the news?"

Although eager to learn why he had come, his question alarmed me for some reason. Perhaps it was because I felt that he was waiting for me to burst out eagerly: "What news?" I lifted my head and gazed at the ceiling, reckoning that my silence might humiliate him. He shifted on his chair and I turned to find his unwavering gaze upon me. I stared back at him for several seconds and then, ill at ease, lowered my head and clasped my hands together. When I looked up again I discovered that he was still watching me, a half smile hovering on his lips. I smiled back.

"What's up?" I asked mechanically.

"Have you heard the news?" he repeated, stretching his neck from side to side.

"What's happened?"

"War's broken out between the Jews and the Arabs."

"When?" I asked, leaning slightly towards him.

"I heard about it yesterday."

He fell silent and lowered his head. I remembered that he had had a neat parting that divided his hair and wondered whether he was now trying to cover up the onset of baldness with a new style. He raised his head.

"The Arabs are demanding a ceasefire."

"The Arabs are demanding a ceasefire," I repeated with an indifference that took even me by surprise. "But why?" I added after a pause.

I believe that my question displeased him, that it pained him somewhat to hear it. He leaned to the left and gazed up at the ceiling. I took two steps towards him, trying to think of something to say. He stood up in turn and moved towards the door.

"But that's not why I came," he said, without looking at me.

"Then why did you come?" I asked after a slight hesitation.

He turned to me, putting his hands in his pockets.

"I have some letters for you."

As I went to take them, he spoke again, his tone quite different.

"On one condition."

In a flash, I realised that he had come to torment me and that everything he had said thus far was simply a preamble for this condition. I considered rushing at him headlong and snatching the letters from his hands but managed to hold myself back.

"What is it?" I asked, backing off.

He followed me, his face mere inches from mine.

"Stop provoking the villagers against me," he said, his wide eyes fixed on me.

"I haven't provoked anyone against you," I cried, seized by a sudden rage.

"Yes you have!" he yelled and I felt his spit on my face. He fell silent for a moment. "I know your tricks," he added, his eyes on mine, "You've spread rumours that I'm working with the merchants from Al-'Ala."

"They're not stupid, even the children know," I said quietly, trying to appease him. "And those letters which you want to give me are of no importance to me," I added, returning to the bed.

"Are you sure about that?"

"Yes," I replied firmly, but knew as soon as I saw his smiling face that I had not convinced him. "You can keep them," I said with complete conviction. "Take them. I know how much you love letters," I added scornfully after a moment's hesitation.

I had hoped that my words would madden him and wanted to see him enraged, but he simply smiled again and sat back down on the chair.

I stationed myself in turn on the edge of the bed, clasping my hands together and watching him as he rubbed his face. Several minutes went by and I could tell that he was thinking neither of my letters nor of the villagers nor of the war between the Arabs and the Jews.

He shuffled his feet and inclined his head slightly: "Do you remember our journey to Goat Mountain?"

He was changing the topic, seeking refuge in the past as I so often did. I was briefly struck by the impression that, deep down, we were one and the same. But, at the same time, I sensed that his question had other, hidden, motives. What did he want?

I plumped the pillow and leaned nonchalantly against it.

"Yes . . . I remember."

He slumped into his chair, stretching his legs. "You may not believe what I am about to tell you but that doesn't matter to me. I was so happy when I first saw you. From that moment, I felt as though your arrival in Goat Mountain would transform my life. This feeling only increased when you took an interest in my grandfather's library and started flicking through his books. You're the first person who's ever done that . . . If you only knew the life I lead in this abandoned village . . ."

He fell silent, as though waiting for a signal to continue. I could tell he had a pressing need to talk and gave a nod of my head, indicating that I was not annoyed. This seemed to comfort him.

"My life here has been tough. Sometimes, I shut my doors and windows just so I don't have to see anyone. I used to love reading, especially epics and histories. But that love soon turned to repulsion and I have never understood why. I began to hate books. Their very shape and smell disgusted me.

"One night I dreamt that I was climbing a staircase of books and that I fell from the top onto a ground covered in icy water. You were the only person who could rescue me. I was convinced of that. I needed someone to help me but you betrayed me, just like everyone else."

"I betrayed you?" I interrupted in astonishment.

"Maybe you didn't do so on purpose but you betrayed me. When you found out I was writing a report on you, you were angry with me without even trying to understand why I was doing it. I had to write it. What else can I do in this miserable village other than write reports?"

I sat up straight and gazed at him in bewilderment. He rubbed his hands together and stood up, looking towards the door.

"I must tell you that I am stubborn," he said. "My grandfather was too," he added as though to himself.

I left the bed and went over to him.

"But I don't understand. What . . ."

"I don't care about anything anymore," he interrupted, turning towards me.

Then, taking the letters from his pockets, he threw them to the floor and left.

5

Soon enough, the residents of Goat Mountain forgot all about the merchants of Al-'Ala. Ismail, meanwhile, kept his promise, and bought their potato harvest every year. When one of the farmers dared ask him for a higher price, however, he grew violently angry and threatened to call a meeting in which he would refuse to purchase any more of the villagers' potatoes.

In the space of a single year, Ismail's house transformed. It suddenly contained luxurious furnishings previously unknown in Goat Mountain: tables with metal legs, chairs of different shapes and sizes, a large wooden desk, plush carpets, stained glass lanterns, a double bed, a wardrobe with a full length mirror and a new radio whose echoes reached through the windows of every house at night. Three rooms with large bay windows were added, constructed by builders whose skills were renowned throughout the neighbouring villages. The men were assisted by four manual labourers who, after completing the rooms, were armed with rifles by Ismail. He announced that the government had appointed them to guard Goat Mountain.

The men began to patrol the village streets, armed with old-fashioned rifles that Ismail had inherited from his grandfather. The children ceased their evening games and the farmers returned home before sunset, refraining from their usual nightly gatherings. Little by little, the guards imposed their rule over the village and the villagers grew accustomed to their presence, particularly as Ismail began to delegate many of his tasks to them: recording new births, settling disputes, organising meetings and buying potatoes.

Around that time, Ismail also ordered his guards to dig a wide grave for his grandfather beneath the mulberry tree. He then recruited men from neighbouring villages and sent them in search of his ancestor's remains in the barren ground around the carob tree. The search operation lasted three days, during which Ismail maintained daily contact with the diggers by means of a celebrated horseman whom he had personally selected for the job.

Every day, the horseman brought the workers maps that Ismail had sketched with the utmost precision the night before. He informed the villagers there were many men at work. They slept in large tents and sang, danced and laughed merrily at night.

When Ismail learned that the diggers had discovered the remains, he shouted with joy and began preparing a great celebration. His joy, however, was short-lived, and, during the burial, his sorrow was profound. Some of the villagers even believed it to be sincere.

Several days after the burial, I began receiving letters that warned me not to grow lax in my professional duties and called upon me to respect the codes of teaching. At first, the letters upset me and I would reread them at home in the evenings, thinking of my mother and of her high hopes for me. Gradually, however, I grew immune to them to such an extent that when I received my letter of dismissal I felt nothing.

★ ★ ★

The teacher who replaced me resembled a clown. He had a flat, snake-like head and the tufty white beard of an aging billy goat. When he spoke his thin lips protruded and his scarlet tongue poked out. He also had a terrible stutter and struggled mightily to utter the simplest of sentences.

The children spent his entire first day in uncontrollable fits of laughter. The new teacher appealed to Ismail for help and he dispatched his guards into the village. They made a round of all the houses, warning the men of what would befall their children if they did not cease their taunts. This, however, proved futile.

Not only did the children continue to laugh but their mirth began to spread. All it took was for one child to smile and the whole class would erupt into peals of laughter that echoed through the school walls and across the village.

Driven by curiosity, the men began to gather at a short distance from the school to catch a glimpse of what was happening within. Little by little they too succumbed to laughter. Rumours began to circulate, claiming that Ismail himself had laughed so long and so hard he had contracted a throat infection and been confined to bed. It was said that one of his guards had spent an entire night flat on the floor, contorted by mirth.

At first, the teacher stood his ground. Each evening he would saunter through the village streets, his hands clasped behind his back. The children would sneak along behind him and fling themselves to the ground whenever he turned, despite being convinced that he couldn't even see well anyway. The teacher's nightly wanderings soon began to lessen and then ceased altogether. He would halt at the mulberry tree and walk round and round it like a bull at the mill. Then, one day, he abandoned the children and locked himself in his room. The villagers hurried to visit him, assuring him that what had happened would never occur again and begging him to return to work. Then Ismail visited him, threatening to write a report.

At first, the teacher's response was limited to various obscure utterances rendered incomprehensible by his stammer. Then he fell completely silent. His silence continued for three days after which the villagers were forced to break down his door. They found him hanging from the ceiling, his eyes popping alarmingly from his head. He was buried in the village graveyard and, to this day, not one of the residents of Goat Mountain knows his name.

★ ★ ★

One morning, the guards began moving about the village as if engaged in particularly intense activity. They strode swiftly from house to house, announcing that an important meeting was to take place at sunset beneath the mulberry tree. Raising my head, I saw them approaching in two short lines, rifles on their shoulders and heads erect as though they were participating in a military parade. I stood watching them with an interest that soon turned to unease when I realised that they were, in fact, heading for me. After drawing to a halt, one of them marched up. Contrary to my expectations he appeared rather well-mannered. He greeted me and delivered his news before falling back into line and retracing his steps with the others.

When I returned home the streets were deserted, for the sandstorm had begun some time ago. In no hurry, I walked slowly, intoxicated by my solitary existence in a silence broken only by the occasional cry of a child or the braying of a donkey.

A thronging crowd swarmed beneath the mulberry tree. The setting sun cast its rosy hues over the ground and, as I gazed across the peaceful fields, I thought of how yet another day had gone by.

For the first time it occurred to me that my life might end there and that I could die in Goat Mountain, buried in its graveyard and lost to oblivion like that poor teacher. My insides clenched at the idea and I tore myself from such musings, gazing absently at the sun as it sunk further into the west. How beautiful it was! Everything passes on, swept along by the current of life, as the saying goes.

I cast my gaze into the distance. The ground stretched forward to the horizon where the endless and terrifyingly pure expanse of the sky began. What were all those people doing, gathered beneath a mulberry tree three centuries old?

Who are these people? I suddenly wondered.

I have no idea how Ismail orchestrated his sudden arrival, but a murmur swept swiftly through the gathering and there he was, standing in the middle of the crowd, changed beyond all recognition. His eyes were bulging and his drooping lower lip was redder than ever. I had the impression that he must be suffering from some serious illness and, for the first time, I pitied him. So this was my nemesis. In a sudden flash of insight I wondered if, after all, it was not an illusion that I was battling.

I ran my gaze across the crowd, huddled on the ground like a herd of slumbering goats, then returned to Ismail, scrutinising his face in search of some mysterious essence, which had struck me the first time I saw him but which I had not fully grasped until this very moment, and then the realisation of it suddenly flooded through me like water into a sleepy desert village.

Who was this man ... and what did he want? I contemplated his pale, thin face with steadily increasing emotion, heedless to the words he was speaking. His image began to grow hazy in my eyes, his features melting away until all I could see was a tall white spectre standing rigidly amidst the crowd as though held from the sky by invisible threads.

6

Outside, the darkness was so thick that my eyes could barely penetrate the gloom while everything around me was plunged into a heavy silence. I lay sprawled on my bed, gazing up at the ceiling. I had just finished a book that I had already read once before. As I rolled over I felt it beneath my stomach. It had a white cover, and was devoid of images. I prefer books without images, books that give free rein to the imagination. When I received my letter of appointment my mother wept with joy. My father doubtless still dreams of a dazzling light illuminating the fields and a magic carpet carrying him off to strange new lands.

I became absorbed in the light cast by my lamp. As I gazed into it, the faces of dead friends began to materialise before my eyes, friends with whom I used to swim in pools left by the first rains of autumn. Together we would hunt for green frogs with gleaming eyes and scoop up tortoises, which we sold on Thursdays to merchants from distant villages. Omar, who had a weakness for raw onions, had drowned. That was the first time that death touched me. We were in the middle of a flooded valley waiting for big waves that we would dive into. Clutching my hand, Omar laughed, his eyes shining with unbridled joy. Then suddenly his hand slipped from mine and he was swept off by a wave. I guess that he must have been carried onto the rocks where his body decomposed, sand covering his bones and wild plants growing over him.

I felt a pain behind my eyes, closed them, then opened them again. Raising the mirror, I examined my face. In spite of the feeble lamplight, I could clearly see my features and my bloodshot eyes. Would my mother recognise me? I had spent months away from my family in a village run by a tyrant under the guise of a mysterious entity called "government" and in the name of a heroic act that took place two centuries ago. Was this situation reality or merely an illusion? And why did these farmers do nothing, content to live off their potatoes? Their children were intelligent and they sang songs in the fields as their bodies perspired. At the close of the farming season, they gathered in their crops, cleaned their homes, circumcised their boys and went to the forests to collect wood for the coming winter.

I was in despair. Ismail was my enemy and his guards roamed the village freely. For the first time, I considered the possibly that Ismail was silently plotting my death. Who would prevent him from doing so? He was an intelligent man and his odd behaviour was merely a smokescreen for his murderous intentions. He had only to send out one of his guards at night to accomplish the deed. There is nothing more horrifying than a human being shot by a hunting rifle.

I do not want to die. The sun that rises after I am gone would be more beautiful than all those that have gone before. The springs too would be more radiant. I know now that death is approaching. Only a few days separate it from me. Perhaps less. In order to live we must die – I read that in a book once. But I am scared. I am cornered and hopeless. What will my mother say? Did my father toil away for all those years so that I would end up like this? I will be buried here, beside that poor teacher. Or perhaps I will not be buried at all. Omar was not buried. But what difference would it make anyway? I want to live, travel and love. I am neither an adventurer nor a hero. I came here by chance and by chance I met Ismail.

I heard a rustling outside, followed by the pounding of endless feet upon the ground. "I'm ready for you," I cried in confusion. I rushed to the lamp and extinguished it. There they were, right in front of my house. I could see each and every one of them, carrying hunting rifles, their faces veiled. Why were they moving so quickly? I stood in the middle of the room, ready and waiting. Bolting the door, I propped my mattress against it, determined to block their entrance, to resist them with every ounce of my strength.

I strained to hear but nothing broke the silence. Where had they gone? Were they laying an ambush? Why had everything suddenly gone quiet? I walked slowly to the door and listened intently, alert to every movement. I gently pushed the door open and poked my head out. The night was impenetrably dark as though in tacit solidarity with death. Closing the door, I lit the lamp, returned the bed to its place and collapsed onto it, shutting my eyes and curling up like a wounded animal. The book had fallen to the floor. I thought of its blank cover, the cover that let my imagination run free ... Blood was trickling from my right hand but I did not attempt to stem the flow. Drops spilled onto the blanket and I counted them ... one ... two ... I was calm. I relished the sight of my blood. "This is my blood. This is my blood so drink from it."

A cock crowed in the village and another followed it a few moments later. The chickens were waking. The earth was beginning another turn. I delighted in that glorious, age-old sound. I had thought it possible that I might never hear it again. I listened to it as though for the first time. How wonderful life was! I resolved to tell everyone. But first it was time to sleep.

7

Goat Mountain was Goat Mountain no more.

I am certain that the villagers still remember how the events of that day unfolded. In the morning, everything was as normal. The heavy rains of the previous week had brought a slight chill to the air and the ground, saturated with water, had changed colour. With the arrival of an elderly teacher the children returned to school and, just like their fathers, became somewhat enamoured of his beautiful wife who never seemed to stop laughing. The farmers went out to the fields to examine their potato shoots, working their fingers into the soil to determine how deeply the water had penetrated. I had not left my bed and lay stretched out like an icy corpse awaiting burial, staring blankly into the room and, every now and then, reliving the fear that had grown steadily worse throughout the previous night.

The news spread quickly. Dogs barked, cows lowed and the children dashed from the school, sprinting towards the gate. Numerous groups of ironsmiths in bizarre outfits had descended en masse into the village, arriving from across the country to construct a gate which Ismail claimed would be one of the biggest in the world, if not the biggest.

That day, Goat Mountain was plunged into a commotion the likes of which it had never seen before. Its streets were filled with the banging of hammers, the rasp of spades and the grinding of drills and metal bars. How many smiths were there? Some of the villagers claim that it was over one hundred while others put it at less. But what truly astonished them all was the speed with which the workers moved about among the piles of steel rods strewn across the ground, avoiding hammers, nails and screws, and moving nimbly between the neatly ordered black forges where fires blazed, sending clouds of blue smoke curling slowly up into the sky.

The residents of Goat Mountain flocked to see them. The men left their fields and the women abandoned their homes. They did not fully grasp what was happening but were determined not to miss a thing. As for the children, they did not return to school. When the new teacher came looking for them he in turn was mesmerised by the sight and ran home to fetch his wife. In bewildered silence, packed together like a flock of whirling birds, the villagers observed the strange men moving with such alacrity between the piles of metal without once faltering or colliding. Each knew which path to take and which task to perform. They were like bees inside an enormous hive. From time to time, a murmur ran through the crowd of villagers, accompanied by the occasional shuffling of feet.

The gate was completed shortly before sunset. Ismail arrived accompanied by his guards, and walked slowly through to the ecstatic applause of the ironsmiths. When he disappeared, the villagers pressed towards it, swarming through in a great, shouting mass.

Little by little, the place emptied of all but a few stragglers who remained rooted to the spot, contemplating the gate in solemn silence. The sun went down, the houses and fields grew quiet and the gate melted into darkness.

The next day, the teacher devoted the first part of his lesson to a discussion about the gate. As he was in full flow, listing the benefits brought by its construction, one of the students interrupted. "It frightens me," the child piped up, looking around at his classmates. His words incensed the teacher who barely managed to keep from striking the boy before sending him away. After a long silence, he continued:

"Goat Mountain has changed. We can now say that it has become a city. This is no exaggeration. It is the truth. You are still young and do not know the nature of cities. I, however, have lived in them for many years and can tell you all about them. I know them well. I know their streets, their houses and their trees.

"What is the difference between them and Goat Mountain? Nothing. Absolutely nothing. When you grow up, you too will visit these cities and discover that they are no different from your city. You will remember my words. I can say that with absolute certainty.

"You will say: 'How right he was, that teacher.' Yes, that is what you will say."

In the fields, one of the men mopped sweat from his brow.

"Where did they get all that iron from?"

"The government. Must be from the government."

They remained in silence for a while longer. Then suddenly one of them broke into song:

> *Oh friend*
> *My mouth has grown quite dry*
> *Persuading Fatima*
> *To love me*
> *As I love her*
> *After a pause, the other responded:*
> *Between these mountains*
> *Curls of smoke rise high*

They continued singing. When one of them fell silent the other would take up the refrain. Their voices drifted out through the noontime silence, filling the village.

Throughout that week, my mind was constantly on my family. For a long time, they had been absent from my thoughts but the letters that Ismail had given me dragged me down into a sea of memories. Whenever I was alone familiar faces would appear before me. My mother's smile and my father's eyes, shining with boundless joy. Sadness would sometimes engulf me, followed by feelings of failure and disillusionment.

I left the village behind and plunged into the fields. The woods lay before me but I was heading nowhere in particular. I simply wanted to walk, to be alone. As I crossed the fields, I felt as though I were in the midst of an obscure world that was slipping constantly through my fingers like drops of quicksilver. The path dropped suddenly downwards. I paused for a moment, absently contemplating the rosy hills that stretched off into the distance, before descending for the first time into the wide, sandy expanse of the valley. On my right, lean cows moved slowly about in a meadow, flicking their tales from side to side. On my left, a Bedouin, wiry and muscular, was forging his way up a steep trail, striking at the undergrowth with his stick, his voice raised in song. As I listened intently to his words the Bedouin's voice began to stir up images from my past: a child taking sheep to pasture, ripping plants from the ground or running down a long, narrow track. Beneath the weight of these confused emotions, I felt a sudden, powerful affection for the Bedouin, as though he were singing for me and me alone. The Bedouin, however, disappeared into the woods, his voice gradually fading until I could hear it no more.

My feet sank into the clean, white sand of the valley. I pulled off my shoes and felt grains of sand trickling between my toes. I continued walking, driven by a powerful desire to pursue the Bedouin. His voice had completely overpowered my senses, drawing me to him as though by magic. I had never heard a voice so pure and beautiful.

The valley, growing suddenly deeper, began to curve sharply around. The sand disappeared and the path grew steadily rockier. I pulled my shoes back on and left the valley behind, climbing a small hill and descending the other side into a hollow dotted with pools of stagnant water. I stopped once more, straining to hear the Bedouin's voice. Everything was silent. I chose a suitable spot to rest and dropped onto the ground. It was late afternoon and the sun was sinking into the west. I stretched out on the ground, closing my eyes and, for no apparent reason, began to think of Ismail when suddenly I heard the voice again, a faint echo in the distance. I jumped to my feet, listening closely, and felt an immense joy overwhelm me, lessened only by the thought of the great distance and the unknown obstacles that still separated it from me.

Having identified the direction from which the voice was coming, I sped off in frantic pursuit, breaking into a run and paying no heed to the ground before me. Jagged rocks and thorny plants tore at my feet without breaking my pace. The Bedouin's voice possessed me to the very core of my being. I sped over hill after hill and eventually circled back into the valley. The further I ran, the clearer the voice rang in my ears.

Reaching the meadow where I had earlier seen the cows, I drew to a halt. Bruises were blossoming on my feet. I sat down once again and listened to the voice, which now cut clearly through the air, dispelling all thought of my battered feet. Every fibre of my being was alert and I felt as though the whole universe was contained within me. I smiled, like a child who has finally got his way. The Bedouin was close . . . he was right there . . . and this time he would not slip away . . . I would get him.

Suddenly the voice disappeared and a desolate silence descended over the vast, empty landscape. I shook my head as though waking from a slumber and spun round scanning the horizon in every direction. Where was he? My body was eager to dart forward in pursuit but I did not know where to go. I stood rooted to the spot and my exasperation turned to fury.

"Bedouin!!" I called, "Bedouin!!"

My voice echoed through the valley before being swallowed up by the surrounding wilderness. I slumped to the ground and pulled my shoes off with a mechanical gesture, stretching my legs out before me. As I examined my bruises, the precariousness of my position dawned upon me for the first time. Feeling abandoned and alone, I was seized by a desire for revenge, swiftly succeeded by a strong sense of self-loathing. As I thought of the Bedouin, the image of Ismail holding forth beneath the mulberry tree materialised before me. Had the Bedouin heard him speak?

I stretched out on the ground and closed my eyes. The pain in my feet began to ease and a gentle breeze blew, cooling the sweat from my body. The sun was close to the horizon but I estimated that there was still a good hour left until sunset. I stood up and continued onwards, moving painfully slowly across the meadow and down into the valley. I halted before an immense ravine packed with dense vegetation, and contemplated it for some time, unable to banish the image of snakes and scorpions, the sight of which I usually cannot stand. I was, however, determined not to give in, to expend every ounce of strength to capture the Bedouin. Arming myself with a long stick, I plunged in, striking the undergrowth to left and right. Before me, quails and small birds took flight while mountain hares scampered for cover. I delighted in the sight of their hasty retreat.

All of a sudden, the path grew narrower and was completely obscured by a tall tangle of plants. Grabbing them in both hands, I bent them to left and right and managed to open up a rough path. Numerous tiny scratches covered my hands but I did not slacken my pace, forging forward until I emerged among jagged rocks which I began to scramble across. Halting briefly, I leaned on my stick and called out once again: "Bedouin!! Bedouin!" As before, my voice echoed back at me before disappearing into the surroundings.

The clouds had changed colour and the ground behind me glowed red. Darkness was spreading over everything. Tossing my stick aside, I began to clamber up the wall of the ravine. Sometimes I would slip down and tumble back to my original position. Although shaking with exasperation I did not let despair overwhelm me. I was determined to escape the ravine before darkness fell and I was left stranded and alone. My trousers ripped and I heard the sudden howl of a wolf. I moved cautiously, keeping close to the rocks and occasionally pausing to skirt around a patch of soft, claylike ground.

Finally, I emerged from the ravine and peered anxiously around. Darkness lay thick on the ground and I could see nothing. I stood numb with shock and not knowing what to do. The howling of wolves increased and the Bedouin had disappeared. I longed for release. "There is no hope," I said aloud. "The Bedouin has betrayed me and I must return to Goat Mountain."

The path rose and fell. As I navigated a small hill, a cold wind blew over me. The sky must have been densely clouded. In despair, I crouched down and drew my knees to my chest, blowing into cupped hands to conjure up the slightest bit of warmth. A sudden gust of wind stirred the earth around me and I felt grains of sand stinging my face. I curled up tighter, burying my head between my knees. I began to caress the earth with both hands, scooping up a handful of soil which I squeezed between my fingers before bringing it to my nose. The smell of earth. How wonderful it was! The Bedouin knew that smell well. Where had he gone? Perhaps he was in his house at the bottom of the slope or behind that hill, stirring a fire with a dry stick.

9

Of the few dreams that visited me during my time at Goat Mountain, there was only one that I remember clearly. It was truly remarkable. There were three of us: me, the Bedouin and a coachman, an old man with a short white beard. We were in a blue carriage pulled by a lean horse through wide, empty streets that were covered in a layer of dust. From time to time, the carriage stopped and we would peer out, contemplating the doors of city houses.

The next day, my back ached as I tossed and turned on my mattress. Stretching out my hands, I examined the many scratches that covered them. Although it was past noon, I felt overwhelmingly drowsy. I leaned forward a little to glimpse the sky. It was clear but for several tiny clouds.

After wallowing for a few moments more I got out of bed and washed. Contemplating my beard in the mirror, I decided to leave it, then left the house.

I had nothing to occupy my time during that period. My renewed desire for reading had completely vanished and I visited the villagers, but rarely. At first, they were persistent in their invitations but, sensing my discomfort, they let me be, and left me completely alone. I guess that the sudden change in my behaviour must have shocked them but I remained certain that they had not abandoned me. Occasionally I felt as though they were treating me like an invalid in need of affection.

As the day grew hotter, I walked towards the fields, pulling off my shoes and continuing barefoot. Relishing the warmth beneath my feet, I felt as though I were taking revenge on the cold of the previous night. I began a long circuit of the houses, studying them as though seeing them for the first time . . . or the last. Ismail's house soon appeared, vast and white like a fortress looming over the modest dwellings that surrounded it. It had been freshly whitewashed and a guard was outside, chopping wood next to a large stable where cows shuffled, their heads buried in mangers. What was Ismail doing? I pictured him at his desk reading one of his grandfather's books or sprawled out on his spacious bed, studying his toes. Then, with a smile, I remembered that he hated books and could barely stand to look at them.

I had seen him only once since the inauguration of

the gate. The sun had still not fully risen but I could see my surroundings clearly. There was Ismail, walking away from me, his back straight and his head held high. Watching in astonishment, I was seized by the same strange intuition that had gripped me the first time I saw him. Every now and then he would stop, shake his hands and continue. He was not far away, only a few metres separated me from him. I wanted to catch up with him and overtake him, not to annoy or taunt him for I bore no hatred towards him that morning, but simply because I had been seized by a selfish, childlike need, an impetuous desire which I had to satisfy. As I drew near, he turned slightly towards me, perhaps sensing my presence. I hesitated for a moment and then continued. Drawing parallel, I turned to look him straight in the eye before overtaking without a backwards glance. I detected no emotion on his face but could clearly see that his eyes were bloodshot, as though he had had no sleep at all. A few moments later, I felt nothing but derision at myself, bitterly regretting my action.

I turned back and began dawdling among the village houses. In one of the courtyards, black chickens were pecking at the ground in search of maggots. On the doorstep of another house an old lady was scratching her bare, flabby thighs while at her side a woman plaited the hair of a little girl who was weeping mournfully. As I studied her face, trying to guess the reason for her tears, a small boy emerged from the house, rubbing his eyes. From his stumbling gait, I could tell that he had only recently awoken. He said something to his mother that I could not make out. In response, she pointed straight ahead without taking her eyes from her daughter's head. The young boy walked a few steps forward. His slender form was stark naked, his small penis dangling between his thighs. Turning his back to me, he crouched down and spread his legs. A gentle trickle of reddish brown faeces began to ooze from his body. Horribly embarrassed, I quickly averted my gaze and left.

By the time I reached the shop the sun was at its highest. I do not know why my feet guided me there. I was not particularly well acquainted with the owner but had always felt that he did not really belong in Goat Mountain and that the only thing that tied him to the villagers was the fact that he sold them their daily groceries. Greeting me with unexpected warmth, he prepared to serve me, then realising that I had not come to buy anything in particular, he pulled up an old chair for me and sat down on the floor beside it.

The shop was not big, with only two sets of shelves, one of which held tins, cartons and cakes of soap and the other bags of sugar, flour and spices. Every now and then the shopkeeper glanced towards me as though waiting for me to speak. I had the impression that my visit had rather thrown him.

"It's very hot," he suddenly said.

"Yes, it's very hot in summer here," I replied, nodding in agreement.

The view was spectacular at that time of day. From where we were sitting, the village houses spread out around us and I tried in vain to define the colour of the earth beneath them as it shifted in the afternoon heat. I am always intrigued by strange indefinable colours, the colour of the potato being one such example.

A child was running towards us from behind the houses. I watched him as he approached and drew to a halt. He was panting and his face shone with beads of sweat. The shopkeeper accompanied him inside. I heard him shouting but remained quietly in my seat as though nothing had happened. A few minutes later, the child emerged, carrying something that I could not identify. He walked a few paces with his head bowed, then broke into a run.

As I watched his retreating figure the shopkeeper returned to his place.

"Business is bad these days," he said wearily.

"Why?" I asked, with my eyes still on the boy.

"Because no one pays."

A long silence ensued during which I imagined that

he was thinking of his dinner. "No one pays. No one ever pays," he repeated.

"There's no way out of paying. They'll all pay eventually," I said, attempting a smile as I tried to alleviate his dark mood.

"Never," he interrupted me sharply, "I know these people well. I've been dealing with them for ten years."

He stood up and entered the shop. I considered returning home but was deterred by the thought of the solitude that awaited me there. Twisting around, I looked towards the shopkeeper standing in a corner with his back to me. When he turned I saw that he was eating something. Our eyes met and he smiled, then returned to where he had been sitting and lay flat out on his stomach, still chewing.

"Do you know Ismail well?" I asked, gazing at his bare feet.

From the sudden jerk of his head I could tell that my question had taken him by surprise but he still answered me, swinging his upturned feet back and forth.

"Yes, I know him. I've known him for a good while." He turned to look at me as though gauging the effect of his words upon me. "Ismail is a great man," he added, "his name has spread throughout the surrounding villages and soon he will be elected as a Member of Parliament."

"Member of Parliament?"

"Soon, inshallah."

"When?"

"I don't know. I've also heard that he is going to buy a car. It'll be the first car in Goat Mountain." He chuckled briefly then added, laughing: "But he won't be able to drive it."

"He'll hire a driver."

"Hire a driver! What's the point of owning a car if you can't drive it?"

The shadow cast by the shop was spreading gradually across the ground. The shopkeeper rolled over and began shifting himself forwards until he found the shade, then, folding his arms behind his head, he fell asleep. After only a few minutes, however, he raised his head.

"Did I sleep long?" he asked, rubbing his face.

"About five minutes," I replied in amusement.

"I didn't sleep well yesterday," he said, entering the shop, then emerging from it again a few minutes later. "I had a terrible dream."

I could tell that he was waiting for me to ask about it but I said nothing, despite the pleasure I usually derive from hearing people relate their dreams. In that intense heat I felt no urge to evoke anything related to the night.

He took a few steps towards me, his eyes on mine.

"Everyone says you're going to get married," he said.

"Get married!"

"Yes. To the daughter of al-Bazi."

I jumped to my feet.

"The daughter of al-Bazi! Who told you that?"

"Everyone."

I returned to my seat and the shopkeeper settled into the shade once again. Several long moments went by during which a thousand thoughts raced through my mind.

"Has she consented to this?" I asked after a slight hesitation.

"I've heard that she's in love with you," he responded without looking at me, "Only this month she refused another offer."

"But no one's ever . . ."

"Her father asked me to talk to you about it," he interrupted me, "he says that she's totally out of control and will only have you."

Khadija, daughter of al-Bazi. Yes, I knew her: a round face with wide black eyes. But why me?

Goat Mountain. What a village! Exquisite potatoes, a man living on sweet illusions and women silently consumed by passion.

10

The sky was clear and blue and, as usual at that time of day, the heat was oppressive. In one of the fields three dogs ran downhill, chasing their way through coffee-coloured furrows, while an old man moved slowly forwards, bending over a wooden plough pulled by a lean horse.

A blue truck arrived in Goat Mountain, rumbling along the streets and cutting through the silence with a deafening roar. At the wheel was a corpulent man wearing sunglasses, laughing heartily and waving his hand, greeting every child or stray calf that wandered along his path. The vehicle had stirred up thick clouds of dust and in its wake the cows began to low, the dogs bark and the chickens squawk. Women leaned their heads through windows and doorways while men abandoned their work in the fields and stood watching the truck in the distance as it headed through the village towards the school, exactly as the villagers had expected it would. Ever since the first meeting in its courtyard, they had come to see it as an official place, the centre of all that happened in the village.

Slowly, the truck approached the mulberry tree until it was almost touching the trunk. It was an old truck, its wheels spattered with specks of mud. The driver got out and contemplated his surroundings, shaking the dust from his clothes. He was short and his most distinguishing features were two bushy eyebrows that cast his small eyes into shadow. His baggy trousers and straight-legged gait gave him the air of a retired colonel. Walking up to the mulberry tree, he placed both hands caressingly on its trunk and raised his head towards its branches before returning to the truck where he began talking with two women seated in the front. In the school, the teacher and his pupils were glued to the windows, watching events unfold in stupefied silence.

From time to time, the driver looked left and right, then down at his watch as though waiting for someone. Suddenly his raised voice pierced the unbroken silence of the courtyard. Neither the teacher nor the pupils could understand a word he said. He was speaking with an astonishing rapidity, bobbing his head up and down and gesticulating with both hands. His voice mingled with the voice of one of the women in the truck. The teacher and children remained motionless as though watching a particularly riveting play in the theatre. Abruptly, the short man and the woman fell silent. The driver leaned his head against the truck window while the woman got out and began walking away, her head bowed low. She was slender, her blond hair was in plaits and two large hoops were hanging from her ears. As she drew near the school, she lifted her head and, seeing the teacher and pupils, retreated a few steps and stood looking at them in astonishment. After a few moments, she returned to the truck. The teacher, a smile on his lips, did not take his gaze from her. The woman and her companion looked down from the truck window, laughing and whispering to one another while the driver walked briskly across the courtyard towards the houses.

When school ended, the children shuffled calmly up to the truck and formed a circle around it. One of the women began to sing. Her voice, low at first, swelled out into the surroundings. The pupils edged ever closer, encircling the truck in motionless silence until the teacher came to usher them away. They stumbled off, scattering in all directions and melting into the village streets.

★ ★ ★

The news shook the village, spreading rapidly to east, west, north and south, as any unusual goings-on generally did. Ismail's guards were mobilised: they barged uninvited into houses and marched from street to street. "Goat Mountain has become a city," they cried. "The band that's arrived is proof! It's one of the most famous bands in the capital."

The usual quiet which blanketed Goat Mountain at night transformed into an excited hubbub. Angry voices rose into the night air, calling, shouting and wailing. Exasperated men cursed their women while neglected children wept. In one of the fields, a pack of teenagers stood debating the number of women in the band. One of them swore that he had seen five of them as the truck passed by, all beauties with round faces and wide black eyes. Another insisted that there were only three, two small and one tall and pale-skinned. A third claimed to have seen only one, long-haired woman.

Suddenly a coarse voice roared out, reverberating through the fields:

"Don't miss out! Tonight you are all invited to a great celebration! Don't miss out!"

The party venue was lit by large lanterns placed in tin cans. Multi-coloured lamps hung from the mulberry tree and a wooden stage equipped with microphones and musical instruments had been erected in front of one of the school doors. The driver clambered onto the stage, joined a few moments later by the two women. All movement ceased, all talk died away and all eyes were on the stage as the villagers strained to catch every second of the spectacle. As usual, Ismail appeared suddenly among the crowd, as if rising from the ground. He walked slowly towards the stage, shrouded in mystery, looking left and right and smiling occasionally as he clasped outstretched hands. He stopped in front of a child and leaned down to kiss it, asking the name of the mother and father, grandmothers and grandfathers. When he reached the stage, the band members began to clap and the villagers followed suit, applauding long and hard. Ismail walked around the stage, waving both hands in greeting to the residents of Goat Mountain. One of the guards then leapt onto a barrel and began shouting in a rough voice: "Long Live Ismail! Long Live Ismail!" The villagers took up the refrain in an enthusiastic babble, their discordant voices clashing. After the guard had jumped back down the chanting faded away until, with a gesture from the driver, it ceased altogether.

Ismail was wearing a blue suit and tie. This was the first time that I had seen him dressed so smartly. He appeared elegant and relaxed in the lantern light. I felt a twinge of pain. This was the occasion he had been dreaming of. He was revelling in his victory. This was his party. A gate, guards, lanterns, a stage, a band. Farmers applauding him, crowning him king. Having made sure that all eyes were on him, he took a paper from his pocket and began to read:

"Today is a momentous day in Goat Mountain, a day

which will go down in history and live forever in our memories."

His voice was strong and clear. His eyes shone and his face appeared paler in the halo of light surrounding him. The image of him standing in a deserted landscape, stirring the sand with his stick, flashed through my mind, followed by other distant memories, surging forward as though stirred up by the spectacle before me.

The sound of rapturous applause brought me back me to reality and I saw Ismail leaving the stage and disappearing into the darkness. The band began to play and one of the women launched into song. At first, the villagers listened in attentive silence but, within a few minutes, they were intoxicated by the music, clapping to the beat and responding to the singer's every gesture. Spurred on, her voice rose to a cry, her hips swaying and her chest heaving as she lifted the crowd to new heights of excitement.

At the end of the song, the woman quickly vacated the stage, making way for her blonde companion who began to dance. As she spun around, her sparkling dress, slit to above the knees, parted to reveal thighs like the fleshless haunches of an emaciated dog. Several of the men, overcome by the sight, began to take turns to dance, each time raising an almighty roar.

The guards rushed over, ordering them to remain calm, but they continued to whoop and roar, threatening to put a premature end to the party. The dancer, meanwhile, was beaming. The men's enthusiastic response had lifted her spirits and her movements grew ever more rapid as she jumped about the stage like a startled chicken, exposing her thighs and swaying her pendulous breasts.

I slipped through the crowd and left the school. A mixture of sadness and repugnance rose within me. I took a short stroll through the silent fields, then returned home and lay down on the bed. I could see the moon clearly through the window. It was full that night. The music, interrupted now and then by shouts or applause, drifted through the window.

Once again, Ismail had taken the people of Goat Mountain by surprise. He must be happy. A band had come to Goat Mountain.

And my father . . . was he still dreaming of a villa, with wide, spacious rooms?

I rolled over in bed and remembered the time I'd spent examining my fingernails and deconstructing my razor. Days were speeding by, time was exerting its influence and the daughter of al-Bazi was in love with me. "Her father has given in and she will only have you." And the potatoes were as good this year as in previous years.

I got up from the mattress and leaned on the windowsill. Alone in the sky, the moon glowed brightly.

I longed to approach it, to draw near it.

I buried my head in my hands and felt my temples pounding. Here was blood, coming knocking at my door. My fingers were icy and fever burned in my face. A sudden thought crossed my mind, something I had never before considered. At this time of night Ismail was alone. I picked up a knife and left.

11

All was quiet when I reached Ismail's house. It appeared larger than normal beneath the bright moonlight. I paused, straining to hear the music in the distance and massaging the blade in my pocket, feeling the warmth of its handle between my fingers. Ismail was alone, like a king abandoned by his people. Tonight, I would become a hero.

This was my test. Killing is a beautiful game, with high stakes. I was astonished by my own rage.

My body was feverish with a fury that had spawned within me during my years in Goat Mountain. Now, it was time to play, time for me to make a move.

I pushed open the door and crossed the courtyard. A pale light shone through one of the windows and to my right a door stood ajar.

Was Ismail expecting me? Ready and waiting for a meeting he had long anticipated. I lurched towards the light as though pulled by a magnetic force. Then, easing the door slowly open, I entered.

I found myself face to face with Ismail as he slouched on his bed like a decrepit bull. He lifted his head and sat up slightly, stretching out his hands as though attempting to grasp hold of something. For a moment our eyes locked. Then he slumped down, leaning against the wall and folding his arms across his chest. He had removed his jacket and tie. I stared at the collar of his badly buttoned shirt. "You came . . ." he said.

I remained silent.

"I was expecting you," he added, and I sensed a note of sarcasm in his voice.

I gazed into his eyes, caressing the knife to reassure myself that it was still there, in my pocket.

"I know you don't like parties. I was surprised to see you at the school. All of a sudden, there you were, a long way from the stage, but I could still see your face clearly. It was the first time that I've looked at you like that. As I gave my speech, I watched you constantly. At one point, you seemed sad and I felt sorry for you," he said, crossing one leg over the other as though shielding himself from a sudden cold wind and then stretching out on his side.

"Every time I see you, you remind me of a childhood friend," he continued, staring at the ground, "the resemblance is striking. I can recall his features now. I can almost see the sparkle in his green eyes. He taught me so much: to ride wild donkeys, trap birds, catch swamp frogs, and larks which we'd pluck and then set free. We used to piss into holes in the ground to chase out black and yellow scorpions, then we'd cut off their tails and use them to terrorise the other children."

He raised his head. "Sit down. Sit down on that chair," he ordered, staring intently at me.

I hesitated for a moment before complying. Later, I regretted doing so, but at the time I convinced myself that sitting down would lull him into a false sense of security, smoothing the way to the deed to come.

Raucous shouts reached our ears. Ismail craned his neck, looking towards the door.

"I can now say that I have achieved my dream. I have accomplished my plans exactly according to schedule. I located my ancestor's bones and buried them in a tomb worthy of them. I constructed a magnificent gate and attracted a famous band to come and perform in Goat Mountain. I know that you don't like the village and deride everything that happens in it, but I am convinced that you will change your mind. You are the only person here who can grasp the importance of what I have achieved, if only you would renounce a little of your egotistical pride. I do not hate you. Sometimes, I even seem to feel a little affection for you. I don't know why, perhaps because you resemble my childhood friend. Sometimes I wonder if his spirit has inhabited your body." His eyes shone and I shifted before his disquieting gaze.

I imagined that he wanted to know my thoughts about what he had just said.

"I don't know," I said, trying to escape his stare.

He hesitated and the questioning look in his eyes vanished. He seemed suddenly distracted. "Yes," he murmured, "Yes."

Then he shook his head and continued:

"What can I do now? My imagination is failing me and the world around me seems to be shrinking. I will admit something to you: having you in Goat Mountain has been a source of great joy to me. This may sound strange but it's the truth.

"For a while, I went on the offensive because your behaviour threatened to compromise my ambitions. But I still reassured myself with the thought that you were here, nearby. For some time, I ordered my guards to watch over you. I didn't want to scare you. I wanted to make sure you were safe. Before I went to bed at night, I would read all the reports that the guards had written about you and imagine what you had done during the day. I would picture you standing in front of a small house, watching a chicken digging for worms. I tried to understand what was going through your mind as you pursued the Bedouin through the valley and what you would say to him if you ever found him. The incident intrigued me and I was distracted by it for days. Why was it so important for you to capture him? The reports attributed it to fear but I am convinced that you are a courageous man and that you enjoy solitude and darkness."

Turning my head, I saw his tie beneath the bed. He must have pulled it off with his right hand and let it slip from his grasp, as a book falls from the hand of a dozing man.

"I too enjoy solitude. Any human who fears solitude is weak and worthless. My grandfather would spend hours in silence, shut away on his own. 'I want to listen to the movement of the world,' he would say, stretching out his hands as though performing an ancient rite. 'What do you mean "the movement of the world", Grandad?' 'Hush now,' he would urge, his rough hands falling onto my head and his fingers tousling my hair, 'I can almost hear the beating of my heart. I can almost hear the sound of water absorbed by thousands of trees.'

"I would gaze into his eyes and strain to hear until I made out the sound of a chicken clucking. 'Did you hear that, Grandad?' 'What?' 'A chicken clucking.' In moments like that, he must have wanted to smile. But he never did."

The light from the lantern was fading, almost covered by the glow from the moon filtering through the open window. I began examining its weak flame as Ismail continued in a slow, tired voice:

"Your departure will be my end. I've grown old, as you can see. When I learned that al-Bazi's daughter was in love with you, I rejoiced and hoped to see you marry her."

"It's just a rumour," I replied, and for some reason my tone resembled that of a suspect defending his innocence.

"They say that love is like the wind," Ismail added, heedless to my words, "I've waited a long time but the wind never blew my way."

He rolled over and lay on his back, just as I had found him when I first arrived. He crossed his arms behind his head and fell silent. I had the impression that he had run out of things to say.

I was just wondering if the time had come to kill him when I heard him weeping. I gazed into his face as I approached him and saw tears running down his cheeks.

"You're crying," I said, not out of pity but simply to play the game until the bitter end.

He covered his face shyly with both hands and continued sobbing wordlessly.

I pulled the knife from my pocket and stepped forward.

Suddenly, he took his hands from his face and, seeing me, his eyes widened in fear. He shouted. I plunged the knife into his chest with all the force I could muster.

He clutched my neck and tried to squeeze. I stepped back, pulled the knife away then stabbed again and heard the blade striking bone. A pool of blood stained his shirt. I stepped back as his hands began to loosen their grip on my neck.

As I left, I paused briefly in front of the door, gazing up at the sky.

The moon was glowing and the band continued its lamentable tune.

ABOUT THE AUTHOR

Habib Selmi was born in 1951 in Al-'Ala, near the city of Kairouan in Tunisia, and since 1981 has lived in Paris, France. His writing career started with short stories, which he sent in to a popular Tunisian radio programme called "Literary Amateurs". A number of his stories were broadcast and he was invited several times by the programme's presenter Ahmad al-Lughmani, a well-known and respected poet, to take part in a discussion following the broadcast of one of his stories. At the end of every month, financial prizes were given for the best stories and poems that had been broadcast on the programme that month. One of the winning stories would be selected for publication in the Radio magazine. Selmi won the prize several times, and three of his stories were published.

His first collection of short stories was published in 1977 and in 1986 his second, by which time he had already started on a new experience ... that of writing a novel, the one translated here into English, *Jabal al-'Anz* (*Goat Mountain*). It was published in Beirut in 1988.

Since this first novel, *Goat Mountain*, Selmi has become a well-known novelist with many works: *Surat Badawi Mayyit* (1990, Portrait of a Dead Bedouin), *Matahat al-Raml* (1994, Sand Labyrinth) and in 1999 *Hufar Dafi'a* (Warm Ditches, excerpted in *Banipal 30*). Selmi's fifth novel *Ushaq Bayya* (Bayya's Lovers, excerpted in *Banipal 18*) came out in 2002 and in 2004 *Asrar Abdallah* (Abdallah's Secrets). This was followed in 2007 by *Rawa'ih Marie-Claire* (*The Scents of Marie-Claire,* English edition with Arabia Books, 2010), shortlisted for the 2008-2009 International Prize for Arabic Fiction, and in 2011 by *Nissa' al-Basateen* (Women of Al-Basatin, excerpted in *Banipal 39 – Modern Tunisian Literature*, 2010), shortlisted for the 2012 IPAF prize. In 2013 *Awatef wa zuwaruha* (Awatef's visitors) was published and in 2016 *Bakara* (Maidenhead). His latest novel is *Al-Ishtiyaq ila al-Jara* (Longing for the Woman Next Door), published January 2020.

Banipal magazine has published several excerpts and texts by Habib Selmi, the first being a short story *The Visit* (*Banipal 4*, 1999). Several of his novels have been published in French translation by Actes Sud, including *Le Mont-des-Chèvres* (1999), *Les Amoureux de Bayya* (2003), *La Nuit de l'étranger* (2008, *Hufar Dafi'a*), *Les Humeurs de Marie-Claire* (2011), *Souriez, vous êtes en Tunisie* (2013, *Nissa' al-Basateen*) and *La nuit de noces de Si Béchir* (2019, *Bakara*). There are also three in German translation, two in Italian and one in Malayalam.

ABOUT THE TRANSLATOR

Charis Olszok is a Lecturer in Modern Arabic Literature and Culture at the University of Cambridge and a Fellow of Newnham College. Her work focuses on depictions of animals and land in modern Arabic literature, and her forthcoming monograph, with Edinburgh University Press, is titled *The Libyan Novel: Humans, Animals and the Poetics of Vulnerability* (June, 2020). She has translated and co-translated several works of modern Arabic fiction, including Abu Bakr Kahal's *African Titanics* (Darf, 2014) and Amir Tag Elsir's *Ebola '76* (with Emily Danby; Darf, 2012).

TRANSLATOR'S ACKNOWLEDGEMENT

I would like to thank Margaret Obank and Samuel Shimon, who first introduced me to the world of Arabic literary translation, and to the writing of Habib Selmi. Work on this translation began some years before this publication, with a first excerpt published in *Banipal 59 – The Longlist* (Summer 2017).

OTHER TITLES FROM BANIPAL BOOKS

Mansi: A Rare Man in His Own Way by Tayeb Salih
ISBN 978-0-9956369-8-9 • Paperback • 184pp • 2020
Translated and introduced by Adil Babikir, this affectionate memoir of Salih's irrepressible friend Mansi shows, with humour, wit, and 20th century personalities centre stage, another side to the author, known for his classic novel *Season of Migration to the North*

The Mariner by Taleb Alrefai
ISBN: 978-1-913043-08-7 • Paperback • 160pp • 2020
Translated from the Arabic by Russell Harris. A fictional re-telling of the final treacherous journey at sea of famous Kuwaiti dhow shipmaster Captain Al-Najdi, with flashbacks to the awesome pull of the sea on Al-Najdi since childhood, his years pearl fishing and the industry's demise, and his voyages around the Arabian Peninsula with Australian sailor Alan Villiers.

A Boat to Lesbos, and other poems by Nouri Al-Jarrah
ISBN: 978-0-9956369-4-1 • Paperback • 120pp • 2018
Translated from the Arabic by Camilo Gómez-Rivas and Allison Blecker and illustrated with paintings by Reem Yassouf. The first English-language collection for this major Syrian poet, whose compelling epic poem bears passionate witness to Syrian families fleeing to Lesbos, seen through the eye of history, of Sappho and the travels of Odysseus.

An Iraqi In Paris by Samuel Shimon
ISBN: 978-0-9574424-8-1 • Paperback • 282pp • 2016
Translated from the Arabic by Christina Philips and Piers Amodia with the author. Long-listed for the 2007 IMPAC Prize. Called a gem of autobiographical writing, a manifesto of tolerance, a cinematographic odyssey. "This combination of a realist style with content more akin to the adventures of Sindbad helps to make *An Iraqi in Paris* a modern Arab fable, sustaining the moral such a fable requires: follow your dreams and you will succeed" – Hanna Ziadeh, *Al-Ahram Weekly*

Heavenly Life: Selected Poems by Ramsey Nasr
ISBN: 978-0-9549666-9-0 • Paperback • 180pp • 2010
The first English-language collection for Ramsey Nasr, Poet Laureate of the Netherlands, 2009 & 2010. Translated from the Dutch by David Colmer, with an Introduction by Victor Schiferli and a Foreword by Ruth Padel. The title poem was written to commemorate the 150th anniversary of Gustav Mahler's birth and is based on his Fourth Symphony, the four sections of the poem echoing the structure, tone and length of its movements. It is named after "Das himmlische Leben", the song that forms the symphony's finale.

Knife Sharpener: Selected Poems by Sargon Boulus.
ISBN: 978-0-9549666-7-6 • Paperback • 154pp • 2009
The first English-language collection for this influential and innovative Iraqi poet, who dedicated himself to reading, writing and translating into Arabic contemporary poetry. Foreword by Adonis. Translated from the Arabic by the author with an essay "Poetry and Memory". Includes tributes by fellow poets and authors following the author's passing while the book was in production and Afterword by the publisher.

Shepherd of Solitude: Selected Poems by Amjad Nasser.
ISBN: 978-0-9549666-8-3 • Paperback • 186pp • 2009
The first English-language collection for this major modern poet, who lived most of his life outside his home country of Jordan. Translated from the Arabic and introduced by the foremost translator of contemporary Arabic poetry into English, Khaled Mattawa, with the poems selected by poet and translator from the poet's Arabic volumes from the years 1979 to 2004.

Mordechai's Moustache and his Wife's Cats, and other stories by Mahmoud Shukair.
ISBN: 978-0-9549666-3-8 • Paperback • 124 pages • 2007
Translations from the Arabic by Issa J Boullata, Elizabeth Whitehouse, Elizabeth Winslow and Christina Phillips. This first major publication in an English translation of one of the most original of Palestinian storytellers enthralls, surprises and even shocks. "Shukair's gift for absurdist satire is never more telling than in the hilarious title story" – Judith Kazantsis

A Retired Gentleman, and other stories by Issa J Boullata.
ISBN: 978-0-9549666-6-9 • Paperback • 120 pages • 2007
The Jerusalem-born author, scholar, critic, and translator creates a rich medley of tales by emigrants to Canada and the US from Palestine, Lebanon, Egypt and Syria. George, Kamal, Mayy, Abdullah, Nadia, William all have to begin their lives again, learn how to deal with their memories, with their pasts . . .

The Myrtle Tree by Jad El Hage.
ISBN: 978-0-9549666-4-5 • Paperback • 288 pages • 2007
"This remarkable novel, set in a Lebanese mountain village, conveys with razor-sharp accuracy the sights, sounds, tastes and tragic dilemmas of Lebanon's fratricidal civil war. A must read" – Patrick Seale

Unbuttoning the Violin
Poems & short stories from Banipal Live 2006
ISBN: 0-9549666-2-7 • Paperback • 128pp • 2006
Selected works by poets Joumana Haddad from Lebanon and Abed Ismael from Syria and fiction writers Mansoura Ez-Eldin from Egypt and Ala Hlehel from Palestine. The 2006 Banipal Live UK tour was a partnership of Banipal magazine with the British Council and The Reading Agency.

Sardines and Oranges: Short Stories from North Africa
ISBN: 978-0-9549666-1-4 • Paperback • 222 pages • 2005
Introduced by Peter Clark. The 26 stories are by 21 authors: Latifa Baqa, Ahmed Bouzfour, Rachida el-Charni, Mohamed Choukri, Mohammed Dib, Tarek Eltayeb, Mansoura Ez-Eldin, Gamal el-Ghitani, Said al-Kafrawi, Idriss el-Kouri, Ahmed el-Madini, Ali Mosbah, Hassouna Mosbahi, Sabri Moussa, Muhammad Mustagab, Hassan Nasr, Rabia Raihane, Tayeb Salih, Habib Selmi, Izz al-Din Tazi and Mohammed Zefzaf. Translations are from the Arabic except for Mohammed Dib's story, which was from the French original.